The ArtScroll Children's Holiday Series

Yaffa Ganz

SHAVUOS

WITH BINA, BENNY AND CHAGGAI HAYONAH

Illustrated by Liat Benyaminy Ariel

© *Copyright 1992, 2011, by* MESORAH PUBLICATIONS, Ltd. *and* YAFFA GANZ
4401 Second Avenue / Brooklyn, N.Y. 11232 / (718) 921-9000
Produced by SEFERCRAFT, INC. / *Brooklyn, N.Y.*

SHALOM and *Chag Sameach!* I'm Chaggai Hayonah — Chaggai the Holiday Dove. Today is the 5th of Sivan. That means it's *erev* CHAG HASHAVUOS — the day before the Holiday of Weeks. Shavuos is the second of the *Shalosh Regalim* — the three festivals when all the Jews went up to the *Beis Hamikdash* in *Yerushalyim.* Of course it's also ...

CHAG HABIKKURIM ... the Festival of the First Fruits

CHAG HAKATZIR ... the Harvest Festival

ATZERES ... a Day of Coming Together

Z'MAN MATAN TORASEINU ... the Time of the Giving of our Torah!

"How can one day have so many names?" Benny looked confused.

"It's easy! There are five different names for the day because there are five different reasons to celebrate! A name for each reason!"

"Chag HaShavuos — the Holiday of Weeks — is a funny name," said Bina. "Shavuos doesn't last for weeks. It's only two days long."

"In the Land of Israel, it's only *one* day long," said Chaggai. "But *sheva* means *seven*; and *shavua* is a *week*; and Shavuos comes exactly *seven weeks* after G-d took the Jewish people out of the land of Egypt."

"But what *happened* on Shavuos?" insisted Bina. "Something had to *happen* if there is a holiday!"

"Of course something happened," said Benny. "We received the Torah at *Har Sinai*! Shavuos is *Zeman Matan Toraseinu* — the Time of the Giving of our Torah. And if *that* hadn't happened, we wouldn't have any holidays to celebrate at all!"

וְזֹאת הַתּוֹרָה אֲשֶׁר שָׂם מֹשֶׁה לִפְנֵי בְּנֵי יִשְׂרָאֵל ...

This is the Torah that Moshe put before the Children of Israel ...

"Why didn't G-d give the Torah to everyone? Why did He only give it to the Jewish people?" asked Bina.

"Because the Jewish people were the only ones who wanted it," said Benny. "Isn't that so, Chaggai?"

"It certainly is!" said the dove. "It was like this...."

ashem went to every nation in the world and He asked, "Will you accept My Torah and keep its laws?" But not one single nation agreed. One nation said they would not stop killing; one would not stop stealing; one would not stop working on Shabbos. Only the Jews said "*Na'aseh v'nishma* — we will do whatever is written in G-d's Torah and we will listen to whatever G-d commands!"

When the Jews arrived at Mount Sinai, they set up camp, and for three days, they prepared themselves to hear the Word of G-d. They bathed and changed their clothes. They were careful not to fight or argue or gossip. They studied and tried to make each day holy. And they fenced off the mountain where G-d would speak so that no one could come near.

Finally, early Shabbos morning, on the sixth of Sivan, in the Hebrew year 2448, the Jewish people stood in front of *Har Sinai*, ready to receive G-d's Holy Torah. Moshe climbed up the mountain while all of the nation — old and young, man and woman — stood at the foot of the mountain. There were millions of people. We don't know exactly how many, but there were more than 600,000 men alone. Even the souls of Jews who were not yet born came down to *Har Sinai*. Every Jew who would ever be — each one was present and waiting to receive the Torah.

לא תרצח

You shall not murder

לא תנאף

You shall not commit adultery

לא תגנב

You shall not steal

לא תענה ברעך עד שקר

You shall not be a false witness against your fellowman

לא תחמד ...

You shall not desire that which is not yours....

The world grew very quiet. A great silence filled the air. No one spoke or coughed or even sneezed. The birds stopped singing; the wind didn't blow; the waves in all of the oceans lay still. Nothing moved.

Suddenly, the silence was shattered! The sound of a

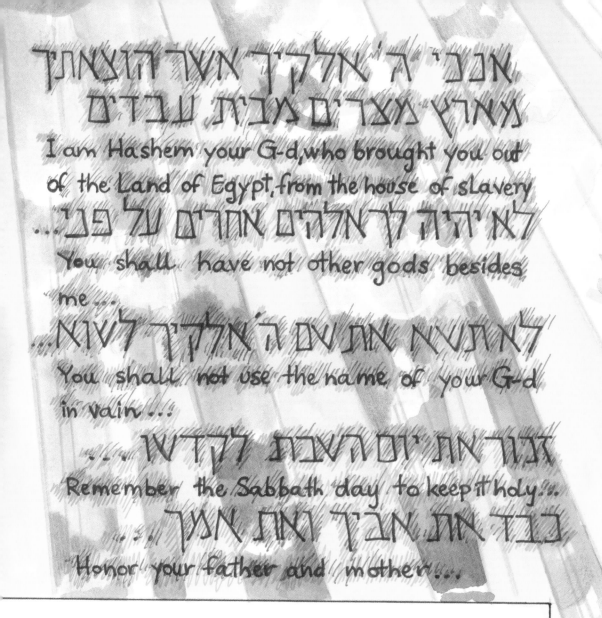

אָנֹכִי ה' אֱלֹקֶיךָ אֲשֶׁר הוֹצֵאתִיךָ
מֵאֶרֶץ מִצְרַיִם מִבֵּית עֲבָדִים

I am Hashem your G-d, who brought you out
of the Land of Egypt, from the house of slavery

לֹא יִהְיֶה לְךָ אֱלֹהִים אֲחֵרִים עַל פָּנָי...

You shall have not other gods besides
me ...

לֹא תִשָּׂא אֶת שֵׁם ה' אֱלֹקֶיךָ לַשָּׁוְא...

You shall not use the name of your G-d
in vain ...

זָכוֹר אֶת יוֹם הַשַּׁבָּת לְקַדְּשׁוֹ ...

Remember the Sabbath day to keep it holy ...

כַּבֵּד אֶת אָבִיךָ וְאֶת אִמֶּךָ ...

Honor your father and mother ...

great shofar was heard and the voice of G-d filled the universe! Mountains shook! Seas foamed and roared! Bolts of lightning streaked across the skies! Giant peals of thunder rolled through the heavens! And the words of G-d turned turned into flaming letters, hanging in the sky.

Benny shuddered. "That must have been scary!" he said.

"It was! The Jews almost died of fright. They were afraid to hear Hashem speak another word!"

"*You* listen to G-d and then tell us what He said!" they begged Moshe. And so they only heard the first two commandments directly from G-d.

"Forty days later, Moshe came down the mountain holding the two *Luchos Habris* — two miraculous stone tablets. All Ten Commandments were carved on them. The letters were carved all the way through — from one side to the other — but neither side was backwards! You could read them from either side — the front or the back. Only G-d Himself could have made such tablets."

"Why did it take so long for Moshe to come down the mountain?" asked Bina.

"He was busy learning the Torah! For forty days and forty nights, Hashem taught Moshe the entire Torah — the *Torah Shebichsav*, the Written Law, and the *Torah Shebal Peh*, the Oral Law."

"It's a good thing he only had to carry down Ten Commandments," said Benny. "If all 613 commandments were on the tablets, they would have been awfully heavy!"

"All 613 commandments are included in the Ten Commandments, and the *Luchos* were *very* heavy, but Hashem made them feel light so that Moshe could carry them."

ina looked at the calendar. "Tonight is the fifti-
eth night since we began counting the *Omer*,
Benny. Did you remember to count them all?"

"Of course I did" Benny looked insulted.
"On *Erev* Shavuos we finish *Sefiras Haomer*, the Counting of the Omer. We counted forty-nine days — seven
full weeks — from the second day of Pesach until *Zeman
Matan Toraseinu* — the time we received the Torah fifty
days later. I said a *berachah* when I counted every night
too!"

"Do you remember what the *Shtei Halechem* are?"

"Sure! The *Shtei Halechem* are two loaves of bread,
baked with flour from the new wheat crop. They were
brought as an offering in the *Beis Hamikdash* on Shavuos
and were eaten by the *Kohanim*."

Bina smiled. "I bet Chaggai would have loved to taste
the crumbs!"

"What are you doing, Bina?" Benny looked at his sister.

"I'm fixing a basket of *Bikkurim.*"

"But there are no *Bikkurim* now! The *Bikkurim* were only in *Eretz Yisrael* and only when there is a *Beis Hamikdash.* They were the first ripe fruits from the *Shivas Haminim* — the Seven Species of wheat, barley, grapes, figs, pomegranates, olives, and dates. They were brought to the *Beis Hamikdash* in *Yerushalayim.*"

"I know, Benny. These aren't *real Bikkurim.* They're just to decorate the table on *Shavuos.* I wish we could have brought real *Bikkurim* to *Yerushalayim!*"

"So do I," said Chaggai. "The *Bikkurim* were a very special mitzvah …

All year long the farmers in the Land of Israel prayed that their crops and orchards and fields would grow. Now the first fruits were ripe, ready and waiting.

As soon as a farmer saw the first sign of a new fruit in his field or orchard, he tied a reed or string or ribbon around the plant and said, "This fruit is set aside for *Bikkurim*."

Then, when the time came for the trip to Jerusalem, he picked the fruits he had tied and put them into a basket. Poor people wove and decorated reed baskets; the rich brought baskets of silver and gold.

In town after town people waited to join the procession. An ox, its horns painted gold and a wreath of olive leaves on its head, led the way. The sounds of flutes and singing filled the air as the people marched through the hills, carrying their *Bikkurim* up to Jerusalem. Thousands of people wound their way through the streets toward the *Beis Hamikdash*. When they arrived at *Har Habayis* each one, even the king himself would put his basket of *Bikkurim* on his shoulder, and march to the Temple. There, each one would give his basket to a *Kohen* and declare:

> ... G-d took us out of Egypt ... He brought us to this place and gave us this land, a land of flowing milk and honey. And now I have brought the first fruits of the land which G-d has given to me ...

❀ ❀ ❀

"Tell us about Ruth," begged Bina. "Megillas Ruth is read in shul on Shavuos. It's a harvest story too."

"Oh, it's much more than that!" Chaggai fluffed his feathers and began ...

ong ago there was a terrible famine in the Land of Israel. Everyone was hungry. Everyone except Elimelech, a wealthy and learned man from the city of Beis Lechem, from the tribe of Yehudah. Elimelech was afraid that everyone would come and ask him for food. So he took his wife Naomi and his two sons and ran away to the land of Moav. "I will return when the famine is over," he thought. But he had done the wrong thing.

The king of Moav welcomed Elimelech. Elimelech was very pleased, but G-d was angry. He was angry that Elimelech had run away from *Eretz Yisrael*. He was angry that Elimelech had not helped his people. Hashem decided that Elimelech must be punished, and soon after, he died. His sons married the daughters of the king of Moav, but ten years later, they died too.

One day, Naomi heard that the famine in the Land of Israel was over. Naomi had never wanted to go to Moav. Now she thought, "Why should I stay here, alone in a strange land? I will return home to Beis Lechem." Her daughters-in-law, Ruth and Orpah, wanted to join with her.

"Go back, my daughters," insisted Naomi kindly. "I am old and poor. Go back to your families. You will find new husbands. I will return to Beis Lechem alone." Orpah cried and kissed Naomi goodbye, but Ruth would not leave.

"Wherever you go, I shall go," she promised. "Your home shall be my home; your people shall be my people; your G-d is my G-d." And Ruth returned with Naomi.

When Naomi arrived in Beis Lechem, the entire town was in an uproar.

"*Hazos Naomi*?" they asked. "Is this Naomi? Naomi was so rich and beautiful. Look at her now! She looks so old! And so poor! Where is her husband? Where are her children?"

It was the time of the barley harvest. The fields were full of workers cutting and gathering the grain. Many poor people were in the fields, too. They collected the stalks that the harvesters forgot to cut, and they picked up the grains that fell to the ground. The Torah calls these *leket* and *shikchah* and says that they belong to the poor.

"I, too, will go to a field and see if I can find grain," said Ruth to Naomi.

Nearby was a field that belonged to the wise and wealthy Boaz. Boaz was one of the Judges of the people. He was also a relative of Elimelech and Naomi. When he saw Ruth in his field, he asked, "Who is this maiden?"

"She is the Moabite girl who returned with Naomi," said the workers. Boaz saw that Ruth was modest and gracious and well mannered.

"Stay in my field, my daughter," he said, "and gather as much grain as you need. You may also join my maidens during their meals. And there is water to drink and a place to rest. No one will bother you."

Ruth thanked Boaz. "You are very kind," she said. "But I am only a poor stranger. Why have I found such favor in your eyes?"

"I have heard of your great love and kindness to Naomi. I have heard how you left your father's house and land to accept G-d's Torah and follow Naomi to the Land of Israel. May the G-d of Israel Whom you have come to serve repay you for your goodness."

Boaz did not forget Ruth and Naomi. He knew that he must help and care for them, too. Even though he was not a young man, and even though Ruth was only a poor stranger from Moav, he married her. Naomi again had a home in Israel and Ruth would become the mistress of a wealthy and honored family. Eventually, the kings of the Jewish people would come from her children.

For Ruth and Boaz had a son named Oved. Oved became the father of Yishai; and Yishai became the father of David *Hamelech*.

"And *that* is why we read the story of Ruth on Shavuos!" said Chaggai.

"It is?" asked Benny. "I don't understand."

"I do!" cried Bina. "The story took place during the harvest, and Shavuos is *Chag Hakatzir*, the Holiday of the Harvest. That's one reason. And Ruth accepted Naomi's G-d and people and land. She accepted the Torah! Shavuos is the day *we* received the Torah, so it's a perfect time to read about Ruth. That's a second reason."

"I can think of a third reason," said Benny. "Shavuos — the sixth of Sivan — is the birthday of David *Hamelech*. David's great-grandmother was called *Imma Shel Malchus* — Mother of Royalty. Do you know who she was?"

"That's easy," laughed Bina. "Chaggai just told us! It was Ruth!"

If all the heavens were made of parchment,
And all the trees in the world were pens,
If all the seas and rivers and lakes were ink,
And all the people of the earth were writers
　　and scribes,
It would still not be enough to describe the
　　greatness and glory of G-d!

s that written in the Torah, Chaggai?" asked Benny.

"No, it's the beginning of a long poem called *Akdamus*. It is read in shul on the first day of Shavuos. *Akdamus* is a poem praising Hashem, His Torah, and His people."

"The words look so funny!" said Bina.

"That's because the words are not Hebrew. *Akdamus* is written in Aramaic."

"Who wrote it?"

"Rabbi Meir ben Yitzchak. Rabbi Meir was the chazzan in the city of Worms in Germany, 900 years ago. His writings were studied by the holy Rashi. Even though Rabbi Meir's son was killed by the Christians in the First Crusade, Rabbi Meir wrote this wonderful song of praise for Hashem. The first word of the song is *Akdamus* and we recite it in shul every Shavuos."

"How sad," said Bina softly.

"No, it's not sad," answered Chaggai. "*Akdamus* is full of happiness and joy. It reminds us that we are Hashem's people and we have His Torah! It gave the Jews strength, and helped them feel proud. It helped them stand strong against a world of enemies. Not everyone is lucky enough to be part of *Am Yisrael* and to have the Torah!"

mmm ... What smells so good?" Benny opened the oven door.

"Kreplach! Imma just put them in the oven. Do you know why we eat cheese kreplach on Shavuos, Benny?"

"Sure! I know three reasons. Kreplach have three corners and lots of things about the Torah came in threes:

- ☐ The Tanach is divided into three parts: *Torah, Neviim, Kesuvim.*
- ☐ The Jews are divided into three parts: *Kohanim, Leviim, Yisraelim.*
- ☐ And Moshe, who was the third child of Amram (who belonged to Levi, the third tribe!), received the Torah after three days of preparation, in the third month, Sivan!"

"And why do we eat dairy foods and foods like blintzes on Shavuos? This is the only holiday we eat dairy foods. Do you know why, Benny?"

"Blintzes? Delicious, sweet, cheese blintzes? I can't wait!"

"But why do we eat them on Shavuos?"

"Because they taste good!"

"Benny! Be serious!"

"I *am* serious. They *do* taste good. But I know another reason too. The Torah is compared to the taste of milk and honey. Shavuos is a *chag* for the Torah, so Shavuos food is milk and honey!"

"Milk and honey are just fine for people, but personally, I still think I'd prefer some of those crumbs from the *Shtei Halechem* ..."

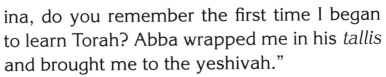

ina, do you remember the first time I began to learn Torah? Abba wrapped me in his *tallis* and brought me to the yeshivah."

"I remember. And he brought an *Aleph-Beis* chart with him. He put some honey on the letters and told you to lick them so that the letters of the Torah would always be sweet."

"Isn't that a nice way to begin to learn Torah?"

"Yes, it is. I didn't lick honey on the letters, but I remember that as soon as I learned the *Aleph-Beis*, Abba bought me a beautiful *siddur*, all my own, with nice big letters so that it was easy to read. And Imma embroidered a *siddur*-cover with my name on it."

It is *Erev Yom Tov*. Bina and Benny are busy decorating the house. Flowers and branches and leaves were everywhere.

"Shavuos is such a nice, green, holiday!" says Bina. "The house looks just like a forest!"

"You mean it looks like a harvest and you'd better start gathering it up quick!" laughed Benny. "When Hashem gave the Torah, *Har Sinai* was covered with a carpet of grass, but I don't think Imma will like grass on her rug."

Bina bent down and picked up a leaf from the rug.

"On the sixth of Sivan, Yocheved put her baby Moshe in a basket. She hid the basket among the tall grasses and reeds growing along the banks of the river. And on the sixth of Sivan, eighty years later, Moshe went up a mountain covered with grass to receive the Torah. Isn't it strange that both things happened on the same day? And that both happened in grassy places?"

"It's not strange at all," said Benny. "That's the way Hashem made it happen. But I think we have enough green in here. If we bring in any more, the house will *really* look like a forest!"

"Hmm ... a green, foresty house ... how nice!"

enny, did you know that Matan Torah was like a wedding? The Torah was the bride; the *Am Yisrael* was the groom; and the ceremony took place at *Har Sinai*!"

"I know. And when Hashem gave the Torah, the mountain rose up high above the people. I bet it looked just like a *chuppah* at a wedding!"

"Well, we always have to take a nap when we're going to stay up late for a wedding, so if you want to stay up Shavuos night to learn with Abba, you'd better take a nap now, on *erev Yom Tov*, too!"

"I will soon. You know, Bina, there is so much Torah to learn that staying up one night is hardly enough. A Jew has to study Torah every single day! I wonder how long it would take me to learn all of the Torah, like Moshe *Rabbeinu*?"

"I don't know, but if you go to sleep now, at least you can get a good start tonight!"

Chaggai yawned. "It's about time for my *erev-chag* birdnap too. So *Chag Sameach* to each and every one of you! From Bina and Benny … and of course from me, Chaggai the Holiday Dove!

And remember …

תּוֹרָה צִוָּה לָנוּ מֹשֶׁה, מוֹרָשָׁה קְהִלַּת יַעֲקֹב
Moshe commanded us to follow G-d's Torah. The Torah is the inheritance of all Jews!

GLOSSARY

Alef-Beis — the Hebrew alphabet
Beis Hamikdash — the Holy Temple in Jerusalem
Bikkurim — the First Fruits, brought to the Temple
berachah — a blessing
chag — holiday
Chag Sameach — Have a joyous holiday!
Chazal — the Sages
chazzan — cantor
Chumash — the Five Books of Moses
chuppah — wedding canopy
Eretz Yisrael — the Land of Israel
erev — the eve of a holiday or the Sabbath eve
Har Habayis — The Temple Mount
Har Sinai — Mount Sinai
Hashem — G-d
Kesuvim — the Writings
Kohen, Kohanim — Priest(s) in the Beis Hamikdash
Leviim — the Levites
Luchos Habris — the stone tablets with the Ten Commandments
mitzvah — commandment
Moshe Rabbeinu — Moses our teacher
Neviim — the Prophets
Pesach — the holiday of Passover
Shabbos — the Sabbath
shul (Yiddish) — synagogue
siddur — prayerbook
Sivan — the third Hebrew month
tallis — prayer shawl
Tanach — the Bible
Yerushalayim — Jerusalem
Yisraelim — all Jews who are neither Kohanim nor Levites
Yom Tov — holiday